PEACE

An odyssey

by

Charles Dada

ISBN-13: 978-1481979818

ISBN-10: 1481979817

CONTENTS

Arrival

The boat rocked alarmingly in the short choppy sea, ultra-marine for as far as they could see. The late spring sun was already hot, and the salty spray splashing in their faces was welcome and exhilarating. There wasn't a cloud in the sky, which was so bright and clear, so blue and vibrant. Behind them, the little square houses of Parga, pink, white, yellow ochre and brown, huddled tightly together in the cleft of the mountains, piling down into the harbour like a stack of boxes.

The argonauts were on their way to Paxos, the island paradise they could see on the horizon in front of them, a perfect place for a sailing holiday. Tourists tended not to stay there, preferring the many villas and hotels on Corfu, from where an occasional pleasure steamer disgorged a few British, Italians, and Germans during the day into Gaios, the main town on Paxos, or on to Anti-Paxos, an even smaller and more enchanting island further south.

Jack looked around at his fellow passengers, all presumably destined for the sailing holiday, having boarded a coach together at the airport. He was pleased to see they were a mixture of all ages, some older teenagers, some in their late twenties or early thirties, quite a few the same age as him, a young forty, and one or two even older men. There was an equal mix of males and females, and they all looked pretty fit and excited by the thought of the adventures ahead. Some of the instructors were there too. The obvious Chief Instructor was a young, but mature, New Zealander, perpetually grinning, wearing shades and a straw fedora. He wasn't going to get sun-stroke! There were two young female instructors, and an older woman with greying hair, slightly expanding about the midriff, but very fit, jolly and friendly, clucking and fussing around them all.

They disgorged off the ferry and dumped their bags onto the quayside in Gaios Harbour. Jack was already impressed by the gay sight of rows of red chairs, blue umbrellas and white tables, and a beautiful, simple, white church with rounded apse right in the middle of the square. They sat down at the nearest tables as the accommodation was sorted out and everybody was told where to go. While they waited, the Chief Instructor, unable to stay idle for a second, suggested a trip round the bay in a water-ski launch. Jack, two other young guys, and a couple of the girls jumped at the chance and piled into the boat. The Chief Instructor at the helm, they revved up and zoomed off, carefully and expertly avoiding the other boats.

Jack looked across the boat at the others. In front of him was a young man with a chin of blue stubble, Peter Fonda type sun-glasses, and curly black hair blowing in the breeze. He wore a chic looking, blue waterproof, open to his navel, black hairs springing out manfully from his chest into the sunshine. Jack saw the golden flash of a medallion nestling in them, hung around his neck on a gold chain. Also around his neck was a white silk scarf, casually tied like a cravat, and blowing in the breeze. Cool and unsmiling, pretending this was the most ordinary thing to do in the world; this guy was obviously full of himself, thought Jack.

On Medallion Man's right was a young woman with a tanned face, flushed with excitement. Her blonde hair, cut short, was blowing about wildly, and she had a big grin on her face. On his other side was a cheerful young man who introduced himself as George, but didn't say much else. He had red hair and moustache, also wore trendy sun-glasses and leant on the rail looking admiringly at Medallion Man. He wore a red and white waterproof, zipped-up tight against the possibility of spray.

The water-skier jumped into the water, and floated awhile, skis pointing into the air, holding onto the line. He rose out of the waves gracefully, as the boat picked up speed, and started to weave around the harbour in graceful arcs. Spray did indeed fly, the horizon spun, mountains flashed before their eyes, a brilliant introduction to the exciting landscape. It was over all too soon and they motored quietly back to the quayside.

There, Sandy, the older Instructor, was waiting for them, clip-board in hand. Two young girls sat beside her.

"Ah! Jack and Nick," she said addressing him and Medallion Man, "You're in the "Villa Stella" up the road with Colleen and Molly here. The two pretty Irish girls blushed and smiled at them, shyly. They all collected their bags and keys and walked in the direction indicated.

They soon found the villa, a welded star atop an iron barred gate, which they pushed open. Jack couldn't believe the beautiful place allotted to them. White walls, with red shutters to the small windows, and a pantile roof welcomed them down the white steps, past olive oil jars and flower boxes full of red geranium, myrtle and pink bougainvillea. They went past the shaded patio, unlocked the front door, and found their rooms. Colleen and Molly were sharing a large double bedroom, with doors opening out onto the courtyard; Jack and Nick were in cool, single rooms at the back, but overlooking beautiful flowerbeds, just as sunny. The ancient furniture was black carved olivewood and very comfortable. There was a lovely tiled bathroom and a small kitchen which Nick immediately raided, crying out that he was starving. He poured everyone a drink of lemonade and passed the glasses around, the height of conviviality and propriety.

They all crashed out on their beds and had a short sleep, until it was time to get up and change for the evening "Welcome" meal in town.

Welcome

By the time it was dark, everyone had assembled in the brightly lit street outside the Instructors' favourite restaurant. Cloth covered tables and cane chairs had been set out along the pavement. Candles glittered, cutlery shone, and glasses sparkled. They all sat down, Jack next to a very attractive young brunette, called Barbara, who seemed to be quite taken with him, though Kenny, a young lad sitting opposite, was more than jealous of her admiring glances.

Soon, dishes of all kinds were piled on the tables by the owner and the waiters: salads, kebabs, moussaka, little fishes, squid, octopus, and rice. Alcohol flowed recklessly: beer, retsina, ouzo, and wine. The Instructors, the Chief in particular, were so friendly, encouraging, and determined that all were going to have the time of their lives. They chatted and laughed, sang ridiculous songs, and were generally very good company.

Jack turned to the girl next to him. "I bet the owner is called Spiro!" he said, confidently.

"Why? Do you know him?" she asked, giggling.

"No, but practically every Greek here is named after St. Spiridion. It's all in 'My Family and Other Animals' ", he replied, showing off his superior knowledge.

"What on earth's that?"

"It's a book by Gerald Durrell. I'll lend you mine, if you like, I brought it with me."

"I don't think I'll have much time for reading," she said, a little drunkenly and coquettishly.

"Why don't you ask him to dance?" Jack suggested, noticing that 'Zorba the Greek' had been turned up to a higher volume on the loudspeakers hanging from the lamp-posts, along with strings of coloured lights, ribbons and balloons.

Lots of people were getting up to dance, and they laughed and shouted as people fell over and into each other, not having a clue as to how the steps were performed. Of course, Medallion Man had to have a go, and joined arms and shoulders with Sandy and the other Instructors who demonstrated gladly.

"I think I'm getting the hang of this!" he pronounced, to general derision.

Jack and Barbara, however, are definitely not getting the hang of it, and are by now dizzyingly drunk and feeling a bit maudlin, for different reasons. He suggested that they go and pick up the book at his Villa. Flattered by the attentions of this older, but not un-attractive, man she hung on to his arm and they walked, rather wobbly, up the road. Outside the starred gate, she pulled him towards her and invited a kiss. But Jack had a sudden pang of conscience and home-sickness.

"I... I can't! " he stuttered. "I already have a girl-friend! "

She looked at him in amazement, went a bright shade of green, and threw up in disgust, dismay and petulance, just missing his feet. She staggered and fell to the floor. Jack was at a complete loss, but fortunately some other girls behind them saw her predicament and rushed over to help. Her friends picked her up and half carried her home to her villa, looking daggers at him. Jack went inside sheepishly, vowing never to get involved like that again, and cursing himself for having ruined a possible friendship in the group.

Sunday

Waking the next day to brilliant sunshine, but a very sore head, Jack decided to walk into town for breakfast and coffee, lots of it. No-one else seemed to be stirring, so he went outside alone. The ancient pink villa next door, set in palm trees and olive trees, looked like somewhere the Durrells would inhabit; the old cottage opposite, like somewhere Zorba the Greek would inhabit, complete with rusting scooter outside the white painted walls, and chickens and goats in the front yard.

He walked down to the harbour, through a little square where vines grew across the frontage of a two-storey house with a full-width balcony; past an ancient olive tree, its twisted, pitted limbs built in to the white painted roadside wall; around another white church with a semi-circular end and brass bells cantilevered from the side; past the small green statue of a boy holding aloft a torch; by the side of gaily painted fishing boats and moored motor boats, the light reflecting off the water so intensely bright, clear and white; and into the central square with the tables and chairs laid out so invitingly.

He sat down and ordered coffee, rolls, butter and jam and ate his breakfast in the open air café, looking at the boats. It was unusually quiet; not many people were stirring. One of the older men from the sailing group strolled up and sat down next to Jack.

"Sore head?" said Stan, his bright face stretched in a wide grin. "Don't worry. It's Sunday today and I don't think much will be happening!"

Jack relaxed in relief, but then became aware of an ethereal singing coming from the other side of the square. A line of young boys and girls from the town and villages around shuffled into the sun, the boys wearing short white cassocks over black skirts; the girls in shorter white dresses, virginal, with flowers in their hair. They were so beautiful and innocent, Jack's heart melted as he sat back to watch the procession go by and into the church. All the mothers and fathers had come out too, dressed in their Sunday best, cooing and aahing appreciatively as their delightful offspring wound past. Jack felt under-dressed in his open-neck t-shirt, shorts and sandals. Even the waiters wore blue shirts tucked into black trousers.

Jack awoke from his reverie and wandered off further round the bay. He came to the Club-House on the beach. Moored in the water by the low quayside were five Wayfarers, the sailing dinghies they were to be taught on. They looked large and substantial, immaculately clean and well presented, jibs furled and mainsails rolled up on the booms. Jack had sailed them before and was really looking forward to being out on the Ionian Sea.

A sixth boat was being worked on by one of the Instructors. Jack went over and introduced himself. Mac was, naturally, Scottish and had been on Paxos since winter, repairing the boats from last season's heavy use. Jack told him about his Mirror, a daft little boat for a six-foot grown man, but it had given him so much fun, introduced him to so many friends, and delighted him with the youth and enthusiasm of his various crews. The great thing about sailing was that you didn't have to speak to people all the time, as you were so engrossed in keeping upright, but you became intimate, moving in unison at close quarters, and trying to achieve a shared goal.

Mac told him about the other Instructors. The Chief, from New Zealand, was called Donald, known to everyone as "Don" or "Skip"; Sandy he had already met; two of the young women were also from New Zealand, Petula, or "Pet", and Kylie; A third girl, Shirelle, whom Jack had not yet seen, was from Australia. Mac loved it here, the sunshine, the sea, the relaxed bohemian life-style in the Club-House, and the ever-changing groups of novice sailors to get to know, entertain and be entertained by. Jack waved goodbye and walked off to explore the rest of the town, buying a straw hat like Skip's and later fixing it with a piece of string so that it wouldn't get blown away.

Rescue

The next day was supposed to be the start of their instruction, but the weather was not really good enough to take the boats out for any hands-on manoeuvres, so an "acclimatising" trip in a couple of Wayfarers was suggested, if anyone was willing to go out in the stiff breeze. Most of the men volunteered, but the young girls and women declined, except for one competent looking woman called Leslie and the carefree girl, Jane, whom Jack had met on the first day in the Water-Ski Launch.

Donning waterproofs and life-jackets, twelve intrepid sailors jumped into two boats. Jack made sure he was with Skip, being joined by Leslie, George, Stan, and Dave - a bearded thirty year-old with a cynical disposition. In the other boat with Mac sat Medallion Man, Jane at his side, Kenny, still viewing Jack with suspicion, Brian, a young lad who so far hadn't said a word, and an older guy that Jack hadn't spoken to yet. They were looking rather more nervous than the people in the Chief Instructor's boat.

Jack competently helped to rig the Wayfarer, unfurling the jib, routing the sheets through the fairleads, tying figures of eight in the ends, and letting them fly, while Skip untied the mainsail and quickly pulled it up with the halyard, straining it tight and wrapping it around a cleat in a few quick turns. The boats were moored stern to and the wind was coming from their forward quarter, though they were sheltered behind the small island guarding the harbour. Skip cast off, telling Leslie to haul on the anchor line, which she did as if she had done this before, pulling it up and stowing it in the bucket at her feet. Jack pushed the centre-board down slowly, cautiously feeling the sandy bottom as it gradually shelved. Skip let the bow fall away and Jack started to ease the jib in. Skip pulled on the main sheet and they were away, quickly building up speed, the others looking on in amazement.

As soon as they were out of the harbour, past the stone berms and large lamps, past the little church on the outer island sheltering the harbour, that they would do well to say a little prayer at, they felt the full force of the wind, and started to pitch and roll in the choppy short sea, the waves bouncing across from the mainland and back again. The boat, inherently stable, was even more so with the heavy load, and seemed to enjoy being out in its element, surging forward and responding totally to every adjustment as they trimmed tiller and sheets. They tacked out towards the mountains, Jack and Leslie taking turns to pull on the jib-sheets, leaning out, with spray lashing their faces, enjoying every minute of it. They gave the others a go, Dave and George rather hesitant, but soon getting the hang of it. Stan sat opposite the Chief at the back of the boat, eyes wide, not daring to move.

They turned this way and that, tried running down-wind and putting in a few gybes, expertly executed by Skip. The other boat followed them south. The waves were getting higher in the confused sea, perhaps four or five feet high. The sea was now a glassy green with spray blowing off the top of the white horses. Suddenly, there was a cry of alarm and a scream from Jane. Looking back, Jack saw Mac waving the tiller he had been mending yesterday in the air. A collection of white faces stared back at him in horror as they began to flounder uncontrollably.

"Get your main down!" yelled Skip, disgustedly, but still grinning from ear to ear.

The main was let down too quickly, and the boom clunked somebody on the head, adding further to the confusion.

"Just run on your jib and catch this line!" shouted Skip again, throwing out a large skein of rope behind him.

They ran in front of the other boat, weaving back and forth, zigzagging with cool jibes, the rope snaking out behind. The others could easily grab it if they leant out a bit, which Medallion Man bravely did, hanging on for dear life and somehow managing to get it through the fairlead on the front of his boat and leading it back to tie around the mast and thwarts. Jack and Skip goose-winged their boat and, towing the stricken craft behind like a disgraced chicken, ran down to the natural harbour of Mongonisi at the foot of the island. As soon as they entered the lagoon, the wind eased and the sea calmed. They pulled over to the beach on the south side, ran up onto the sand and leapt out of the boats, holding them steady, their legs weak and knees wobbly. It had been a magnificent rescue!

"That was close!" laughed Skip, fresh and unconcerned, as he had already planned this escape route in case of trouble. "That'll teach you not to rush repairs, Mac!"

They repaired to the Beach-Hut, ordered calming drinks, and waited for the Jeeps to come to take them back to Gaios.

Capsize Drill

Next day, sailing instruction started. Not before time, some thought, and Skip, after yesterday's adventures, was determined that Capsize Drill couldn't be delayed. But first they gathered around the blackboard and Mac started with a serious warning about "Spiny Normans". These were spiky, black sea urchins, which grew to the size of a tennis ball and lay on the sea floor waiting to trap the unwary and sink their poisonous barbs into someone's foot. It was a two-hour operation to get them all out!

He then explained the various parts of the boat to them, starting the lesson with "front and back", and ending it with "fore and aft". There were a few bemused faces, and a few bored ones, though Mac tried to keep it light with amusing anecdotes. He was still a little shame-faced from yesterday's débâcle and couldn't quite summon his normal enthusiasm.

A couple of boats had already been set up in the harbour, where the water was deep enough. Putting on their life-jackets in the prescribed manner, the aspiring sailors were all taken out in the water-ski launch. In pairs, they were put in a boat and the drill explained again. Some were very nervous, never having sailed before, let alone capsized in a boat, the very thought of which filled them with horror. The first problem was trying to get the heavy boats to capsize at all! They tried rocking as hard as they could, leaning over the side, pulling the sails this way and that, all to no avail. From the launch, Mac demonstrated his secret weapon, and, pulling on the sailing boat's main halyard attached to the top of its mast, he tipped them screaming into the water.

The right way to proceed is to float in the water, the helm grabbing a jib-sheet and throwing it over the side. The crew should hold on to the thwart and push down the centre-board, but not pull the boat towards or on top of them. The helm should then swim around the stern, pushing the bows head to wind, holding on to the main-sheet, and climb onto the centre-board. With the crew floating in the water, parallel to the boat, head forward, the helm stands on the centre-board and leaning out, pulls on the jib-sheet. The boat should slowly rise, the boom and main sail sinking into the water. The turning motion will scoop the crew back into the boat and he or she can then balance the boat, tidy up a bit and help the helm to climb in, if he or she has not expertly stepped in over the side as the boat rights. All very simple!

Of course, what actually happens, as demonstrated successively by the various following attempts, is that nothing ever goes to plan. The first problem is that the boat can completely turn turtle, trapping someone underneath, and losing all their possessions, sandwiches, flasks and spare clothes to the bottom of the sea. Panic! Fortunately, there are abundant lockers in a Wayfarer and everything should be tied on. The unfortunate crew bobbing under the boat will soon realise they can see, and there is loads of air, they just have to swim out from under the hull.

The helm swimming round the stern may hold on to the jib-sheet by mistake and find it's just not long enough. Where is the wind anyway? What wind? Arriving at the bottom of the boat, there is no centreboard to climb onto. Shout! Bang! The centre-board is pushed out and clonks the helm on the head. It is too high! There is no way he or she can climb onto the thin slippery, slidey thing! With a tremendous effort, legs and arms akimbo, a purchase is gained and the helm struggles on to the board. Where's that sheet? Shout! It whizzes through the air and strikes him or her, wet and sharp in the face.

Nearly over-balancing as George caught it, he straightened up and started to pull. His feet slipped, crashed into the hull, and he pivoted gracefully sideways, hitting the bottom of the hull, sliding off the board, and falling backwards again into the water.

Trying again, exhausted by now, he pulled more carefully, and the boat did indeed begin to rise, slowly at first, but accelerating as the water drained off the sails. Jane, was scooped in, but George fell back into the water, the boat rolling over the other way as the crew forgot to balance the boat and she fell, screaming, onto the helm's head, the boat turning completely and trapping them both in eerie silence underneath.

The idea then is to somehow climb onto the up-turned hull, stand on your toes on less than an inch of gunnel rail, hold onto the centre-board, or the slot, and rock the boat until it turns onto its side. Easier said than done. And it's another ducking if, by some miracle, it does come up. Of course, if the water depth is just right, the top of the mast sticks in the sand and refuses to budge. Then it's a case of jumping and pounding on either end until it frees; very difficult.

Molly and Colleen were both far too light to pull the boat up and gave up in disgust. Skip made a mental note to always pair them with someone heavier. Colleen didn't give up altogether though, and exchanging Molly with Dave, tried again until she found her balance in the boat and leaned over to assist him. He just couldn't climb back in; the sides seemed far too high and he pulled and struggled, until Skip suggests diving feet first down into the water and then kicking, rising up quickly, his buoyancy giving him an extra boost over the side. Medallion Man tried the same trick when it was his turn, but promptly pulled Molly into the water and the boat over on top of them again.

They all took their turn, laughing and becoming increasingly confident in the water. It was great fun really, in the warm sea, with buoyancy aids, and the sun beating down. Eventually they all achieved success and, feeling very proud of themselves, were ferried back to shore for a drink.

In the afternoon, after a salad lunch in the square, they went out again, four to a boat, and actually started sailing about, just outside the harbour. There is an instructor in each boat, but Jack couldn't resist showing off and giving everyone the benefit of his knowledge.

"If you watch the luff of the sail, you can trim it easily," he says, confidently. "Push your tiller towards the sail until it just start to crease, or pull it back if it creases too much and loses power."

The Instructor, Pet, looks at him, startled, and smiles indulgently.

"Where do you get to know that?" Dave complains, sarcastically.

"Well, I have got my own boat, a Mirror."

"A Mirror!" scoffs Dave. "That's a kid's boat, like those Toppers!"

"Well, it's all the same idea'." replies Jack, not letting on that he has spent the last eight years sailing Wayfarers, Wanderers, Enterprises and his Mirror on courses up and down England and at his Sailing Club at Rudyard.

Dave has a go, and tries out Jack's suggestion. It does seem to work, and he grudgingly gives him some respect.

They carry on practising, each taking it in turns at the tiller. Jack is impressed as Colleen leans out on the jib-sheet, the only one daring to do so, so far. She had a lovely smile and laughed gaily as the spray caught her face. Jack practiced rolling up and down waves; turning into them as they rose, and falling away, picking up speed, as they rode over the tops and down their backs.

He feels attuned to the boat, tiller extension and mainsheet working in contra-unison, tacking with an expert thumb trapping the sheet as he swaps sides and twists the stick around. This was so enjoyable it was like being in a pleasant dream. He hoped it would never end.

Fancy Dress Disco

After a meal at one of the restaurants in town, Stan told him that the evening entertainment was a Fancy Dress Disco. It was to be held in a tin shack just out of town, up the hill. It seemed there were loads of other young people on the island, though where they were hiding, Jack did not know. It was very dark inside, until the lights started flashing; and smoky with incense and heady substances. The music, from huge speakers and a couple of turntables operated by a swarthy young man in a striped t-shirt and dark shades – how could he see? – was heavy rock and pulsing dream trance. Jack didn't have any fancy dress, but neither did anyone else apparently, at least nothing that wasn't pretty common these days.

Everyone gyrated around, swayed on the spot, or leapt up and down frenetically, shaking themselves into a deeper trance like whirling dervishes. Kenny, Barbara and the other young things joined in energetically. Jack watched hesitantly at first, but was soon persuaded to dance by Leslie, Jane and Gillian, already rocking with Dave and George. Medallion Man was there of course, looking cool in his shades, until Jane swung him round and into the group. He responded quite violently, spinning himself around and around, performing the most acrobatic of steps.

The Instructors were there too and, rather to the annoyance of the other tourists, demonstrated some more Greek dancing. Sandy was particularly lively.

Jack went outside for a drink and to calm his spinning head. He sat at the tables and watched spellbound as fireflies chased each other, winking under the olive trees. The air was warm, and he was feeling a little tired after the day's exertions, and, drunk on ouzo, beer and wine, he wandered back alone to his starry villa.

In the morning, another headache! Trying to find his sun-glasses he couldn't find his coat. It had his wallet in it and, very stupidly, his passport. He hardly ever wore it in the heat of the day, but took it with him last night to the restaurant and possibly the Disco; he couldn't remember!

Not knowing what to do, as everywhere appeared closed and locked up, he ran in a bit of a panic to the Instructors' villa. Here, all of the Instructors stayed in comparative peace and privacy, their only break from the relentless demands of their customers and the busy itinerary. They were all looked after under the watchful eye of Sandy.

29

He knocked nervously at the door which was opened by Kylie, sleepy-eyed and half undressed. He tried to explain, but she let him in to the kitchen, where Sandy was sipping a mug of steaming coffee. She offered him one and he accepted gratefully. Strewn around the room were various items of women's underwear, brochures, lists, books and half-eaten sandwiches.

Jack instantly felt homesick and poured out his troubles to Sandy's sympathetic ears.

"I'm sorry to bother you with this, but I've lost my coat, all my money, my wallet and my passport!" he admitted, shamefacedly.

"Everything! You silly boy! What will we do with you?" teased Sandy.

"I know. It's very stupid of me," he said. "I think I left my coat in the restaurant, but I may have taken it up to the Disco. So, where it is now, God only knows!"

"Don't worry, my dear. Let's give them a ring."

She spends a few minutes on the phone and then informs him that his jacket is safe and sound up at the Shack.

"These people are incredibly honest, you know," she purred. "They would never steal anything, and they are so grateful for the extra income we bring in. It's a very poor place, so it makes it all the more surprising and heart-warming."

Jack thanked her profusely, and, though he was anxious to get his coat and everything else back, he didn't want to leave this warm, comfortable place, and the warm, sympathetic Sandy.

"I'm sorry about that scene at the weekend with Barbara," he said.

"Oh don't worry!" she tutted. "She's not come to any harm, and she shouldn't have got drunk in the first place!" She continued, "But you were very gallant not to take advantage of her."

"Oh, no! I couldn't!" exclaimed Jack. "I've only just found the girl of my dreams at home. I miss her so much!"

Sandy's heart melted and she shooed him out to reclaim his belongings.

He walked up the hill and knocked on the wooden door to the Shack. Sure enough, his jacket was there. He thanked the Greek profusely and offered a reward.

He was waved away brusquely, a smile on the lips of
the old man.

Mongonisi

A day off from the serious work of learning to sail, and most people got a lift in the Jeeps to chill out in Mongonisi. This was a fabulous, relaxed place. A huge, blue, sheltered lagoon at the south end of the island, surrounded by silver white sand, gently sloping down to the water. The sun beat down relentlessly, but with a gentle breeze. There was a Beach-Bar for all the Beach-Bums, picnic tables and chairs. People lounged around with drinks in their hands or lay on the hot sand, sunbathing and turning slowly golden brown. Jack bought a drink, lay down and dozed. After a while, he went swimming to cool off; a gentle breast-stroke, and then floated on his back. This was paradise!

A number of people were trying out wind-surfers, with varying degrees of success. Jack had a go, but was completely hopeless at keeping his balance and kept falling in the water. He also tried snorkelling, but nearly choked as soon as he put his head below the surface of the water. He looked around in despair.

Teaching the teenagers, and other complete novices in the group, how to sail Toppers was the most gorgeous girl Jack had ever seen. Tall, slim, lithe and athletic, and wearing only a very skimpy, red and white dotted bikini, she moved with a grace and precision hard to believe. She demonstrated the various points of sailing on the little boat, balanced on the sand, ducking under the low boom and stretching out, feet under the toe-straps. Her nut-brown body and short, glossy black hair, smoothed to the shape of her head, gave her an Indian appearance.

"Who is that?" Jack asked Mac, as they both stared appreciatively.

"That's Shirelle, our other Instructor!" Mac replied, proudly. "She is from Australia, but originally I think she or one of her parents was from Sri-Lanka."

Her smiling, laughing face, shouting instructions in broad Oz, and her obvious love of, and ease in, the water certainly attested to her present homeland. A beach-peach girl, if ever there was one! Now he knew what he was going to practice!

It was easier and more exhilarating than he had imagined, having previously dismissed the small plastic boats, with their brightly striped triangular sails, as "tea-trays". He was joined by Stan, who was also determined to learn to sail solo, being a bit over-awed by the Wayfarers. Jack demonstrated the finer points and they were soon whizzing around the buoys, with very few capsizes.

Logos

It was blackboard time again. They gathered round at the Club-House, listening intently as Mac tried to explain mysteries such as "Tacking", "Reaching" and "Gybing", and the "Apparent Wind Direction".

"We start off with the wind on our side, and the sails flapping out on the other side," he said, pointing to the diagram. "Pulling them in slowly, our speed forwards will start to increase. As we do so, the wind will appear to move around forwards, heading us. Now, if we don't pull the sails in further, they will back in the wind, and the boat will stall. The sails should now take on an aerodynamic shape and instead of the wind pushing them, they will be sucking them forwards, like an aeroplane wing."

Another diagram. "We will go faster and begin to turn into the wind, pulling the sails tighter, but not too tight, until we are going as fast as we can against the wind, beating at forty-five degrees, although the sail will actually be at about five degrees to the wind. Any closer and the sail will back again, losing power, and eventually stalling."

He gasped to a halt. There was a murmur of bemusement.

"I haven't a clue what you just said!" exclaimed one of the older women at the back. This was Gillian, a very attractive brunette with long frizzy hair teased out into a round mop that must have taken all morning to comb into place.

"Ah. Well, don't worry," said Mac. "All will become clear on the water!"

They jumped into the boats again, four to a boat, and cast off, erratically wending their way in a ragged line through the harbour walls. This time they turned left, to port, and began to reach northwards, hugging the coastline fairly closely, and admiring the verdant hills. The wind was moderate, but the swell on the sea, left over from a storm in the night, was spectacularly huge. Jack thrilled as the boat lifted on to the peak, running down fast into the valley, the boats around disappearing in the ten-foot swell. Sometimes, his heart stopped as they seemed to be charging down on top of another boat and would disappear into the greeny-blue water, but magically they floated up again, like being held aloft on a sheet of transparent plastic film. He felt perfectly safe and secure, confident of the boat, his own abilities, and the increasing skill of the others.

They sailed round a wooded headland and into the bay of Logos opening up before them. The hills on either side, covered in olive and cypress trees, ran down to the water, gradually enclosing them as they ran towards the harbour. However, instead of entering it, as Skip knew it would be pretty full of local fishing boats, they turned into a small cove beneath some trees, coming up gently onto the sandy beach, and jumping out before crunching to a stop. They moored the boats fore and aft, the anchor out behind, the bows tied to the trees. They furled the sails neatly, making the boats ship-shape as they had been told. Skip was an absolute stickler for boat presentation, aware that they were the biggest asset and advertisement for his company.

They walked along the dusty road and Jack looked at the colourful fishing boats, moored bow-to along the quayside. At the end of the quay was a row of shuttered shops and chandlers. He took a photograph of them. They wandered on through the small harbour village, past some apartments and an old Olive Oil factory in ruins, but still charming and photogenic. They walked up the hill, on a white chalky path between gorse and ferns, looking back through the branches of leafy olive trees to the harbour below, tranquil and peaceful, until they came to a ruined windmill on the headland. George stood framed in the stone arched doorway, Dave beside him taking photographs. On the very top of the headland, they gazed out over the sea to the blue mountains of Greece on the other side of the straights, the yellow gorse blooms at their feet nodding stiffly in the breeze. They walked back slowly, reluctantly, with views over the ultra-marine bay; the harbour and the village; the heather-fringed sea; and the inland hills covered in olive trees and cypresses.

Back in the harbour, a meal had been arranged at the local Taverna, eight drachmas a head. They all settled down at the tables, parched and thirsty, relieved by the bottles of beer already set out, and chatted and laughed amongst themselves, so proud to have made a real journey to "somewhere else". Even Gillian had taken to the water like a natural and had performed confidently after a little trial and error. Not a regular tourist spot then, there wasn't much on the menu, just salad and little fishes, but with bread and olive oil, they felt contented, basking in the sun.

Scooters

Another free day: no instruction and no sailing, a welcome change for some. Dave suggested a scooter ride up into the hills. Jack, George and Leslie jumped at the idea, as they all knew how to ride. Starting up the gravelly road, with loose pebbles, hairpin bends, and sudden descents and ascents, explained a lot about the accidents they had heard about, and the arms and legs in plaster-casts and splints that Jack had seen around town.

They came to a church yard overlooking the Erimitis cliffs, and looked around amongst the white marble gravestones. Near the entrance was the gnarled limb of an old olive tree poking out of the ground and protected by a low brick wall. At its forked end, hung an ancient bronze bell. They went inside the small, simple church and, when their eyes became accustomed to the contrast, they were staggered to see an ornate alter covered with brightly painted and gilded icons. They were the best Jack had ever seen, easily competing with those in museums and art galleries. And here they were, unprotected and innocent, a revelation for all to see in the peace and calm of the lonely hillside.

They went outside and took a narrow path through the ferns, the white limestone Erimitis cliffs plunging into the azure sea below. The path became steeper until they came to a rocky plateau, probably the remains of the foundations to an adventurous villa or cottage that had once stood there. There was a flat, rectangular platform of concrete, just the right size for the four of them to spread out their towels, take off their clothes, and lie in the mid-day sun.

Soon becoming hot and sweaty, Jack picked up his camera and wandered down some steps to the sea below, hoping for a cooling dip. There was a small strip of white silica, which scintillated under his feet, and he gratefully waded into the freezing cold water. It was so clear he could see the bottom right out to the foot of the cliffs, where it shelved steeply. He carried on around a corner of rock, holding his camera above his head, and found another little rocky cove, with a small cave worn by the sea into the cliff face.

Walking up onto another even smaller white beach, he had to be very careful where he trod as some of the rocks, broken bubbles of glassy volcanic lava, were razor sharp. He was also on the look-out for "Spiny Normans".

It was a secret paradise here, the light shimmering on the white walls as the ripples reflected upwards.

He was almost acclimatised to the cold sea now, so, putting his camera on a rock, he fell back into the water, and floated on his back, gazing up at the endless blue sky. He spread out like a star in the firmament until, suddenly, he felt a sharp pain on his left arm. He had been stung by a jelly fish, and he thrashed in the water trying to get it off, and making it ten times worse. He quickly struggled to his feet, grabbed his camera, and waded back to the other beach. He teetered over the pebbles and ran up the steps to the sunbathing deck. He rubbed his arm vigorously, until it became numb.

Leslie was lying on her stomach, topless, wearing only her white knickers, at right-angles and close to his towel. The other two young men lay on the other side of her, both wearing their trunks, and getting nicely brown. He took off his wet trunks, and lay down on his towel, his feet a yard from Leslie's head. He lay back, feeling free and liberated, soaking in the warmth as the beads of sea water evaporated. He closed his eyes and felt the sun on his face, a gentle breeze tickling his hair. She peeked at him, but why should she care? He was only a skinny little male thing!

As his body came back to life after the cold water, the pain from the sting became unbearable again. He grunted and rubbed it, asking Leslie if she had any anti-histamine cream.

"You could always try peeing on it!" she suggested, helpfully. "That's supposed to work."

Jack sat on rock and urinated into his hand, rubbing it on his arm. Leslie raised herself up on her elbows, exposing her pointy breasts hanging down, and watched him, concerned.

It works! "That's better. Thanks!" he said, gratefully.

Leslie lay back down, her head resting on her arms, dreaming again about the girls on Gaios beach. No one is bothered by their nakedness; even George strips off his trunks and swims nude in the crystal clear pool below, climbing out and sunning himself on a large flat boulder. Dave, however, declines, more worried about the jelly-fish.

After an hour or so, they begin to feel peckish and thirsty, so they dressed, climbed back up to the road, mounted their scooters, and looked for a Taverna. They soon found shade under vines and an olive tree. They sat at the blue and white cheque covered tables and blue plastic chairs, and tucked in to Greek salad, white bread, beers and ouzo, served by a cheerful middle-aged woman, dressed in black.

"Do you always sunbathe naked?" asked Leslie.

"Well, not usually in public," Jack replied. "But I do have a very private garden back at home, and I love to dash home at lunch-time and just lie in the sun!"

"Well, it's certainly invigorating," said Leslie. "Did you know there's a nudist beach in Gaios?"

"No! Really? I thought we were supposed to keep covered up so as not to offend the locals."

"In town, yes. But the beach is just up around the corner from where you're staying. All the tourists from Corfu go there, the young ones, anyway."

"Hmm… We'll have to check it out sometime!"

"You just want to show your body off and ogle everybody else!" said Dave, cynically.

"And why not?" replied Jack. "I think we've all got lovely bodies!"

Leslie smiled, knowingly, and sipped her ouzo. Too soon, on that magical day, it was time to scoot back to Gaios.

Beach Barbecue

At the weekend – Saturday? – He was losing track of time – A trip on the ferry back to Parga was offered by Skip, to pick up more people and instructors, and take the "weekers" back. Jack and a few others boarded the ferry in anticipation, eager for a change of scene.

Tying up in the busy harbour, they agreed to meet back at the ferry later and wandered off into the crowded squares and steep streets.

The local men sat around in cafés drinking Turkish coffee, but looked at you suspiciously in case you were a Turk! There were no women; they were probably all at home or working. The old men played dominoes and backgammon on rickety tables and old boards. Jack tried ordering a coffee, but no-one seemed to understand him. It was not a welcoming place at all. Soon, though, it was time to wander back and board the ferry again. There were quite a few new faces and Sandy kissed one guy fervently. Apparently, he was an old flame and had re-joined them as another Instructor. His name was Dick, and coincidently was from Manchester.

To welcome the new arrivals, an evening trip to Anti-Paxos on a Caique, a small fishing boat skippered by a local Greek, was arranged for that evening. Dressed warmly and carrying waterproofs, they boarded the little gaily painted boat and stood on the deck, looking around, trying to recognise everybody. The Chief Instructor was there, obviously, still wearing his hat, a broad grin, but not his shades. He was chatting to Sandy and the new instructor, Dick. Jack spotted Leslie, Dave, George, Jane, Gillian and the Medallion Man, but missed Barbara, Kenny and some of the other youngsters. Perhaps they had gone home.

There were a lot of new faces too. A tall young man in a white sweater, blue jeans, and grey pointed shoes; other single women, young and older; and quite a few couples. He was pleased to see Molly and Colleen giggling in a corner.

They approached the tiny island at dusk, the white beach still glowing as brightly as the white-painted bowsprit at the front of the boat. The boat nestled against some rocky steps at the side of the bay and they all disembarked in single file. The Instructors carried out crates of beer, various boxes of food, and other implements. Very soon they had a camp fire and barbecue going at the back of the beach, where there was a Beach-Hut, closed for the day, but with a stone patio, chairs, logs and low walls to sit on. The night grew dark very quickly, and everyone got hold of some beer, sausages and burgers, settling down for the evening's entertainment.

The versatility of the Instructors continued to amaze Jack. Not only were they excellent sailors, teachers, and guides, they could sing, dance, tell funny stories, juggle with flaming brands, and chill out!

Everyone laughed at their antics, particularly Molly and Colleen, sitting on the sand. Nick sat next to Gillian on a log, glass in hand, smirking broadly. At his side was Jane, and George was on her other side. Leslie sat behind on a stone wall with the new young man, by the side of a huge, horizontally fluted olive jar. They had the same hair style, thought Jack, amused. On a director's chair, balanced precariously in the sand, sat Stan, grinning as usual. Everybody else sat around the camp- fire in a circle, listening to the stories and anecdotes, each Instructor in sequence doing a star turn.

They hushed as Shirelle picked up her guitar and strummed it gently. She began to sing a soft, jazz ballad, all trace of her Australian accent gone. It was so beautiful, everyone was in tears when she finished.

The smoke from the fire got in everyone's eyes, and they wiped them, wistfully, while the glowing embers glowed, yellow flowers waved, and the starry, starry sky glittered and twinkled. They were all slowly getting sloshed with the copious amounts of beer being handed around. The entertainment over, they sat around chatting, getting to know each other. Jack met a young couple from Marple, which was near to where he lived. They seemed very friendly, talkative, and looked forward to sailing, though Richard did have a cold and Mary was being very protective of him.

After midnight, the Caique nosed back into the bay, its red and green navigation lights twinkling in the wavelets. A searchlight beamed out onto the steps as it gingerly nudged in and moored temporarily, the skipper holding on to a line. They filed back on board, happy and satiated. A slight mist descended and it became cold and damp. Everyone put on their waterproofs, if they had them, or shivered in the tiny cabin or under awnings.

Jane, Dave, George and Stan sat on the deck against the wooden boarding of the wheel-house, a blanket over their legs. Jack couldn't hear what they were talking about, but George looked up into Dave's face, adoringly. Leslie sat by the wooden bulwark, clinging on to the metal rail above.

She was still holding a beer bottle and grinned at Jack, conspiratorially, her ear-rings tinkling as she put her head back, laughing. Richard and Mary, wearing bright red waterproofs that matched their noses, clowned about as Jack took flash photographs of them all.

The Race

Sunday. Not much going on at the Villa. Molly and Colleen sat outside the kitchen door, a perfect suntrap. Jack noticed the broom beside them; such domesticated girls! Nick walked into the kitchen, bleary-eyed and a little the worse for wear. He made a coffee and played with some cereal in a bowl.

"What you need is some exercise!" said Jack.

"Oh. What do you suggest?" replied Nick, yawning.

"How about a walk along the cliffs to Mongonisi? It's not far, about 2 km."

"OK, it's good fun there. Just give me a few minutes."

They set off in half-an-hour, Jack armed with a sketchy map he had bought with his hat, and they were soon amongst the ferns and bracken of the south-eastern slopes, looking down into the blue water.

"Are you enjoying the holiday?" asked Jack.

"You bet. The sailing's great and the girls are gorgeous!" replied Nick. "But I can't seem to get them interested in me."

"You try too hard. You should just be yourself. Act naturally," suggested Jack.

"Easy for you to talk. Anyway, I don't see you getting very far either!"

"Well, I'm not so interested in that. I'm here for the sailing. Besides, my love's at home, waiting for me to get back. Much as I like it here, I do so want to see her again. I wish she was here, but we both booked holidays ages ago, before we met. She's in Mallorca," said Jack, wistfully.

"Love!" snorted Medallion Man.

Soon they were lazing about in Mongonisi again. Medallion Man challenged Jack to a race in the Toppers. Everyone thought this was a great idea as both had been boasting about their prowess and showing off in different ways. A course and starting line was set up opposite the Beach-Hut. Dick joined in, eager to show off his prowess as the new Instructor, and to impress Sandy. Jack, Dick and Nick sailed around, back and forth, behind the starting line until the starting gun fired.

Tacking across each other, Dick capsized almost immediately. Jack and Nick raced for the buoys in the lagoon. They followed each other round, swapping places frequently, sailing hard, well-matched, both surprised at how fast Toppers could go in the brisk north-easterly breeze.

Medallion Man was ahead on the homeward downwind leg, but a gust caught Jack and he just managed to hang on, creeping to the back his boat, planing, precariously keeping his balance. The gust caught up with Nick, who immediately capsized, his boat rolling forwards stern over bow. Jack raced across the line to cheers from the watchers on the shore. All were impressed.

"This is what sailing is all about," said Stan. "When you see it done properly, you realise it's in a different league!"

Richard and Mary, the couple from Marple, befriended Jack. He was now their hero, as they had been thoroughly disgusted by Medallion Man and his show-off techniques. Drinks were bought all round, and Jack was slightly bemused by his new-found popularity. Even Sandy blew him a kiss, though he would have preferred a smile from Shirelle.

The Round Trip

The following day saw six Wayfarers heading off north from Gaios on the first leg of their "round the island" day sail. There were only four instructors available, so Jack and Nick, being the most experienced sailors of the group were allowed to helm. Richard and Mary elected to go with Jack as the "safest" bet, and they took Brian along too, although he still hadn't said much. Nick's crew were Molly, Colleen and George, quite well-balanced should they capsize! Jack saw Leslie with Shirelle, Stan and Jane, but couldn't see the others from where he was up at the front.

The weather was very pleasant: a light to moderate breeze, with no increase forecast; bright sunshine, as ever; and a relatively flat sea. The latter was quite important as they planned to go into some of the spectacular large caves on the west side of the island, and didn't want to bump their masts on the roof.

They reached all the way up to the northern tip, rounded the headland and ran down into the beautiful sheltered cove of Lakka, turning to port into the harbour, and then tacking up, anchors dropped strategically as they turned, mooring stern-on to the quay-side with many other boats. Furling the sails and making everything ship-shape as usual, they ambled over to the taverna close by, tables and chairs already arranged, following an earlier phone-call by Skip. George sat with Gillian and Skip at one end, chatting and laughing animatedly; Jack sat at the other end with Richard and Mary, Molly and Colleen, who had really come out of her shell and was chortling with laughter. Nick, Dave, Jane and all the rest were there, somewhere in the middle, but it was all becoming a bit of a blur in the mid-day sun and with bottles of beer swilling down refreshingly.

After the usual salads and kebabs and a little bit of a rest, they were off again, rigging their boats and heading out to sea once more. Turning south down the west side of the island, the sea was calmer, as the huge white cliffs rose up above them, giving them shelter, but making it a little tricky to judge the direction of the wind. They came to the staggering sight of the Ortholithos, a huge tooth of white rock sticking out of the sea. They passed between it and the cliffs, Skip leading the way, and began to melt into the folds of the coruscated white limestone. They entered a cave gingerly, paddling in, looking down through the clear water at the white and black pebbles of the sea-bed below. They could almost touch the walls at the far end and it became distinctly gloomy, but with dappled reflections still splashing over the roof.

Further south, was the Blue Cave, which was even more spectacular, with the water living up to its name, and the stone vaults above them, twisting in various directions. Then Jack recognised the Erimitis cliffs and shouted excitedly to George and Leslie behind him, pointing out the sunbathing spot to Richard and Mary.

"I won't tell you what went on there, but it was very memorable!" he said.

There were so many enticing looking bays, all with caves or beckoning white beaches, that he soon lost count, until they came to the sea-canal between the last hill of Mongonisi and a tiny island on the southern tip. The plan was to go through it! It didn't look wide enough for a boat and it was head-to-wind, so they couldn't sail through. Getting out the paddles and leaning over the side, Jack told everyone to pull like mad; there seemed to be a current forcing them back again.

"Go on! Put some welly into it," he shouted to Brian, who looked back scathingly.

"You don't have to shout," he said. "I'm doing my best, and I don't really like sailing, anyway!"

Jack was staggered, but let it go, just smiling at him encouragingly. Soon they were clear and were able to tack again, rounding the headland and running back into the lagoon.

They had a quick rest and a drink before heading back up to Gaios in the Jeeps, leaving the Wayfarers for tomorrow's RYA exams, feeling well-satisfied with the day's achievements. Richard and Mary were ecstatic and they all decided to go out for an evening meal, Stan, George, Nick, Molly and Colleen joining them. Leslie and Shirelle were nowhere to be seen.

Anti-Paxos

While the novices took their final assessments for the RYA exams, the more experienced helms and crew were allowed to sail down to Anti-Paxos on their own. There were only three boats, the most competent helming, but taking turns to steer. They sailed gaily out of Mongonisi, round the headland, past the tiny island and on to Anti-Paxos. In the distance they could see the silver beach where they had had the Barbecue aeons before. The water was crystal clear over brilliant white sand, giving a pale turquoise sea. There was a Cruiser from Corfu moored in the middle of the bay and the German tourists had all dived into the water and swam ashore. Feeling superior, they sailed carefully past and moored their three smart boats in deep water at one side and also swam ashore. First stop was the Beach-Hut and then drinks on the beach as they all sat down to sunbathe.

Two teenage German girls frolicked and splashed in the crystal clear water, their lithe, tanned bodies glowing golden in the bright sun. They were topless and wore the skimpiest of bikini bottoms, but were totally unreserved and uninhibited. Jack walked past, watching them casually, but appreciatively, to take some pictures of the three Wayfarers seemingly floating in the air where they were neatly moored. On his way back to the group, he noticed the two girls had laid out their towels and were lying down on their backs, knees in the air, soaking in the sunshine. Their round, recumbent breasts lay reclining on their chests, brown budding nipples about to burst into the sky.

Later the hardened sailors cruised back to Gaios for an evening meal and drinks in a bar. They chatted casually, reminisced about all their adventures, and exchanged addresses. Tomorrow was the last sailing day; the Regatta! Jack asked Colleen to crew for him, not just because she was the lightest, but because she was so competent, did exactly as required, and was so keen and eager to please. Medallion Man was obliged to ask Molly, which he did with grace, though he would have preferred to go with Jane, who agreed to sail with George. Dave and Gillian made up another boat. Stan crewed for Leslie, and Richard and Mary said they would have a go, though they were not expert sailors by any means.

The Regatta

The Regatta course was laid just outside the harbour in front of the Statue, which gave a convenient start and finish. The six Wayfarers would sail first, only two to a boat, to be followed by the single-handed Toppers.

Medallion Man had a grudge match to win. The course would take them in front of the small island sheltering the harbour and be overlooked by the small white church and lighthouse on the outer island.

They tacked around waiting for the start. Jack counted down carefully, well-used to race starts at Rudyard. Bang! They were off! Both he and Colleen leaning out hard, they shot forwards, shouting "Starboard!" at Nick and Molly, on the wrong tack.

They went immediately into the lead and Jack looked round for the next mark, a large buoy moored in front of the church. Rounding it to starboard, they were off again, tacking towards the distant mountains.

The outer mark was some way off, and Medallion Man had at last got up some speed, shouting at Molly to lean out. Jack rounded the mark again, gybed, and started to run back to the Harbour mouth.

Nick's gybe was a bit dodgy and they nearly went in, but he recovered and, shouting like a cowboy, tried to catch Jack up. He and Colleen were now faced by the slower boats tacking towards them. There were one or two hairy moments, as some crews didn't know what tack they were on, or what the Sailing Rules were, anyway! Most boats just decided to keep clear.

Jack had to take quick evasive action for one though, getting very close to the rocks, and slowing him down. Nick and Molly overtook them, a triumphant grin on Medallion Man's face. Jack called for "Water", and crept out again, racing for the line and the second lap.

Tacking back to the church buoy, he soon caught up with Nick, but didn't quite manage to get round first. It was neck and neck as they tacked hard back out to the mountains, Jack and Colleen reaching the outer mark first and gybing round it quickly and expertly, Colleen helping to balance the boat.

Again, they charged down-wind. This time, all the other boats kept out of the way, watching in amazement as the two protagonists shrieked past. This leg was hairy as the wind had become more unpredictable and gusty. Jack pushed the centre-board down to give some stability and charged towards the harbour mouth for the last time. Turning to port, he reached down to the line, tightening up again to beat up to it and over. The gun exploded in their ears, and then again a few moments later, as Nick and Molly crossed.

Jack had kept face, with much help from Colleen, and he leaned forwards and kissed her. She smiled ecstatically, not really sure whether they had won, but pleased it had gone so well. Medallion Man sailed past, a face like thunder, but he managed a grin as Jack waved to him.

A prize-giving ceremony was arranged at the Club-House in the evening and they all sat down for their last meal together. Sandy handed out the prizes. Jack and Colleen received all the first prizes; Medallion Man and Molly were runners-up. The Topper sailors were each awarded a prize and a kiss from Shirelle, and all the RYA certificates were handed out. There was much jollity and stupidity, but lots of fun, laughter, and good feelings towards each other.

Skip gave a little speech and said how much he had enjoyed the fortnight, pleased with such enthusiastic sailors and no mishaps.

The Real Prize

There was much sadness at leaving. Saying goodbye to Skip, Mac and Sandy on the Ferry at Parga was quite emotional. Jack shook Skip and Mac's hands, complimenting them on making these two weeks an absolutely unforgettable experience. Sandy kissed everybody, but kissed Jack on the mouth harder than he had expected. He was sad to leave, but looking forward to home, and seeing his girl-friend again.

They flew back to London, leaving Medallion Man, George, Dave and Leslie at Heathrow. He kissed Leslie ardently; she still had a twinkle in her eye. Sharing a taxi and going back on the train to Manchester with the couple from Marple, he could hardly bear to lose contact with the last of the group, but boarded the train back home from Manchester to a lonely, empty cottage. His girl-friend wasn't back from Mallorca until the following weekend.

He went at last to Manchester airport to greet her off her plane, tanned and frizzy-haired, a wide Cheshire grin on her face, so pleased to see each other again.

They made love passionately as soon as they got back home. Later they exchanged experiences and looked through his slides. Jack told her about his exploits and showed her his many prizes, none though as terrific as the one sitting beside him. He was intrigued by the motley collection. There was a white ceramic mug, with red and blue sails painted on the side; a soft, red, embroidered, Greek skull cap, complete with golden tassel; and a red and pink, woven wool bag-come-purse, also with tassels, not at all the thing a young man would wear over his shoulder; bought perhaps for a girl? As he opened it, a folded scrap of paper fluttered out.

Opening it, he read, "*I love you!*"

"I don't understand," he said, puzzled.

"Well, I think I do!" she said, kissing him affectionately.

THE END

Also by Charles Dada:

MY FRIEND, JACK

Read the rest of Jack's progress through the swinging sixties, the soporific seventies, and the reawakening eighties, as he tries to find that special person who will be his life-long lover and companion.

Will he ever be successful, or is he doomed to eternal disappointment? Whatever the outcome, he always stays optimistic and has lots of fun trying!

OODLES

The world is approaching catastrophe.

It is mostly controlled by by the international conglomerate, Oodles. Can The Founder save the world from its fate?

Join the adventures of the Substitutes and the Rebels as they too try to head off disaster.

What is the future of Mankind; and what is its past?

UNDERMINED

Follow the thoughts and adventures of Jenny, David, Marc, and Arthur as they set off on a coach tour of Andalucía.

Events are not quite as they appear from the start, and Jenny's vivid imagination is taken over by disaster as she descends into a maelstrom of horror and sexual fantasy.

Only love and her own strong recuperative powers can save her from an eternal void, resurrecting her in a shocking denouement. The novel is an explicit exploration of sexuality, and the identity forming crises of childhood and religion.

CHARLES DADA

Charles Dada writes from his own experiences of people and places, but with a large element of fantasy thrown into the mix. His principle concerns are the pursuit of love, fulfilment, and the game of chance and coincidence in everyone's lives.

Contact him at dadachuck@gmail.com

16607474R00039

Printed in Poland
by Amazon Fulfillment
Poland Sp. z o.o., Wrocław